# 1,2,3 suddenly in CHINA
## The Sacred Flower

Cristina Falcón Maldonado
Illustrations: Marta Fàbrega

BARRON'S

FT. WALTON BEACH LIBRARY

On Martin's eighth birthday, his grandfather gave him a tiny package and said, "I've been an explorer all my life, and now it's your turn to see the world. Here is the key to my secret storeroom where you'll find everything you'll need."

In the secret storeroom, Martin found maps and equipment as well as his grandfather's travel album and a strange necklace that came with these instructions:

*ATTACH STOREROOM KEY TO NECKLACE. PUT NECKLACE ON.*

*CLOSE EYES. NAME DESIRED DESTINATION OUT LOUD.*

"Amazing!" Martin said. "I can go anywhere in the world!"

He attached the key to the necklace, put it on, closed his eyes, and said . . . "CHINA!"

Then one, two, three, suddenly . . .

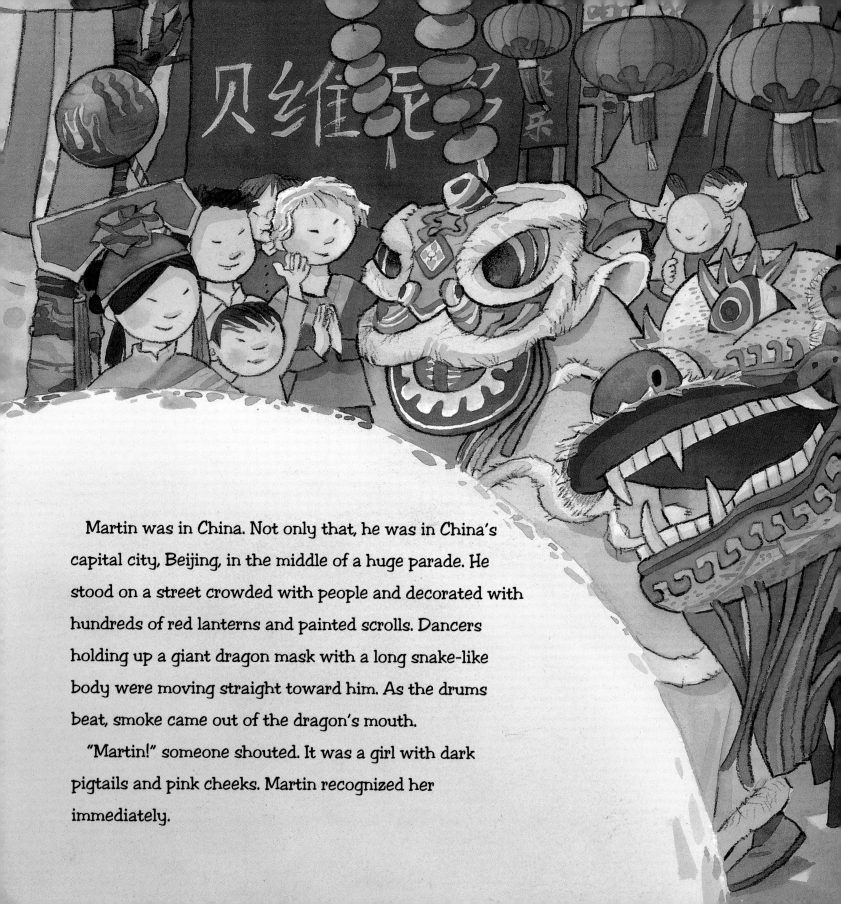

Martin was in China. Not only that, he was in China's capital city, Beijing, in the middle of a huge parade. He stood on a street crowded with people and decorated with hundreds of red lanterns and painted scrolls. Dancers holding up a giant dragon mask with a long snake-like body were moving straight toward him. As the drums beat, smoke came out of the dragon's mouth.

"Martin!" someone shouted. It was a girl with dark pigtails and pink cheeks. Martin recognized her immediately.

"You're the girl in the photo in my grandfather's travel album!" Martin said.

"*Ni hao*, Martin! Hello!" the girl said. "You've arrived just in time for the Chinese New Year Festival! This is the Year of the Dragon!"

4-5

The girl took Martin's hand and began running down a side street.

"My name is Wang Li Meixiang," she explained as they ran. "In China the family name comes first. You should call me by my first name—Meixiang."

"Where are we going, Meixiang?" Martin asked. "And could we walk there? I'm getting out of breath."

Meixiang smiled. "We're going home. My whole family is waiting to meet you."

They walked for almost an hour until they reached a small house, also decorated with red lanterns and scrolls. A boy was waiting for them in the doorway. Martin recognized him from the same photo.

"Ni hao!" the boy called, waving his arms. "I'm Meixiang's cousin, Zhou."

Martin grinned and said, "Now I'll speak my first words in Chinese: Ni hao, Zhou!"

6-7

Meixiang introduced Martin to her mother, grandmother, and grandfather.

"Now we must do three important things to celebrate the New Year,"
Meixiang said. "First, we have to make lots of noise to scare away Nien, the
terrible monster."

Martin's eyes opened wide. "A real monster?" he asked.

"Long, long ago," Meixiang's grandfather explained, "Nien would appear on the first day of the New Year and devour crops, animals, and people, especially children. One year some villagers discovered they could scare Nien away with the color red and loud noises. So now we celebrate every New Year with lots of red and lots of noise."

"And the second thing we do," Meixiang's mother said, "is to give children red envelopes with good luck money inside." She handed the three children their red envelopes. She also gave Martin a letter.

"And what's the third thing?" Martin asked.

"We eat lots of great food!" Zhou shouted.

8-9

After the family and Martin finished eating and watching fireworks outside, Martin opened the letter he was given.

"It's from my grandfather!" he whispered, looking at the drawings and maps. Then he read the message:

Dear Martin,

You're off on a great adventure. Ah, China—what a marvelous place, full of new sights and sounds, smells, and tastes. Remember this: he who takes no risks does not achieve what he desires.

Love, your grandfather

P.S. The sacred snow lotus marks a journey's end.

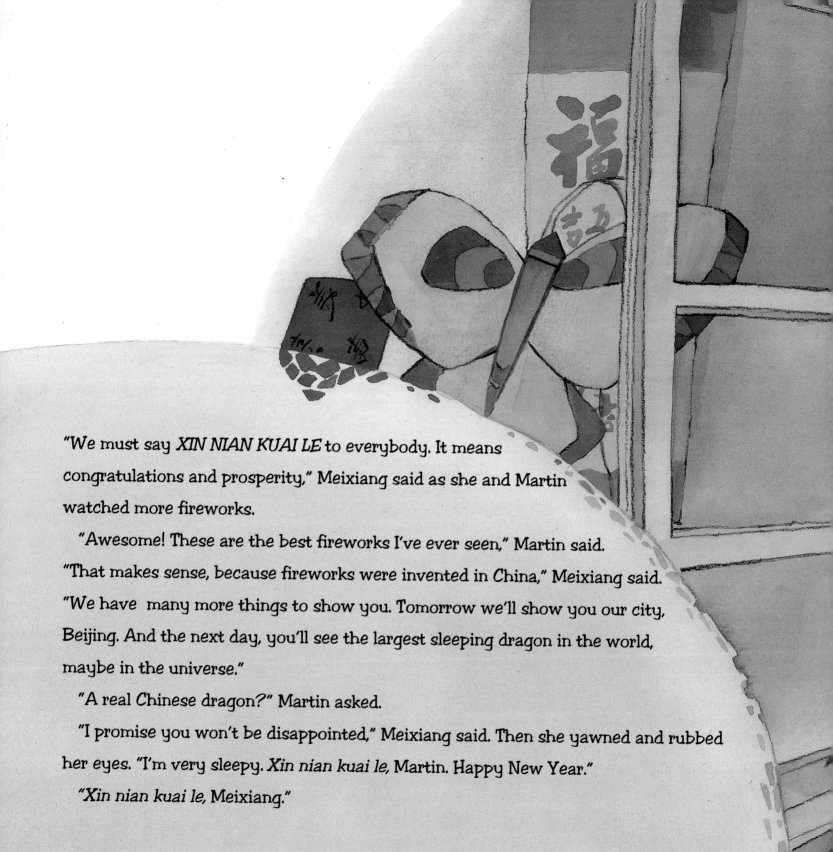

"We must say *XIN NIAN KUAI LE* to everybody. It means congratulations and prosperity," Meixiang said as she and Martin watched more fireworks.

"Awesome! These are the best fireworks I've ever seen," Martin said. "That makes sense, because fireworks were invented in China," Meixiang said. "We have many more things to show you. Tomorrow we'll show you our city, Beijing. And the next day, you'll see the largest sleeping dragon in the world, maybe in the universe."

"A real Chinese dragon?" Martin asked.

"I promise you won't be disappointed," Meixiang said. Then she yawned and rubbed her eyes. "I'm very sleepy. *Xin nian kuai le*, Martin. Happy New Year."

"*Xin nian kuai le*, Meixiang."

"I've never seen so many bicycles!" Martin said as they walked to a park near Meixiang's house early next morning. "Or so many people in a park!"

"Beijing is a huge city," Meixiang said. "More than twelve million people—and there are almost as many bicycles and rickshaws!"

"Are all those people in the park exercising together?" Martin asked.

"Yes, they're doing *tai chi*," Meixiang explained. "It's one of the traditional Chinese martial arts. Come on—let's try it! I'll show you what to do."

In an outdoor market, Martin stopped to watch a man writing in Chinese.

"He's using a brush and ink," Martin said. "It's beautiful."

"Chinese letters are called ideograms," Meixiang said. "He's writing in Mandarin, which is the kind of Chinese we speak in Beijing. More people in the world speak Mandarin Chinese than any other language."

"How many ideograms would I need to learn in order to write it?" Martin asked.

"Oh, only about . . . six thousand!" Meixiang said.

14-15

"The Forbidden City is like another city inside Beijing," Martin said.

"You're right," Meixiang said. "It contains many imperial palaces. It's called the Forbidden City because only the emperor and his household were allowed inside. Those who entered uninvited paid with their lives."

"All the gardens and temples are beautiful, too" said Martin. "What is that blue and green tiled wall with the dragons on it?"

"That's called the Nine Dragon Screen," Meixiang answered. "It marks the entrance to a palace built by one of the emperors for his retirement."

"What did you like best?" Meixiang asked when they got home that evening.

"Well . . . everything!" Martin said. "The Forbidden City, Beihai Park where we saw the lake and another wall with nine dragons. And then for dinner, we had one of your most famous foods, Peking Duck, and the . . . the . . . z . . . z . . . z-z-z-z."

"Sh-sh, everyone," Meixiang whispered. "Martin is asleep."

16-17

"Wow! The Great Wall of China is huge and goes on forever!" Martin said. "And it does look like a gigantic sleeping dragon, stretching across mountains and valleys."

Meixiang's grandfather, whom everyone called Grandfather Wei, had taken Martin and Meixiang to northern China to see the Great Wall.

"It's about 4,500 miles long," Grandfather Wei said, "the longest structure ever created. It was built, expanded, and rebuilt over many hundreds of years."

"Who was the wall supposed to keep out?" Martin asked.

"Invaders from the North," Grandfather Wei answered.

"I've heard that the Great Wall can be seen from the moon," Martin said.

"For a long time, people thought that was true," Meixiang said, "but today scientists know that it's not." She sighed. "Too bad—it made a good story."

Back in Beijing, Martin and Meixiang went to
the famous Donghuamen Night Market where every
kind of food—from the well known to the strange—was sold.

"First I'll show you the most interesting stuff," Meixiang said. "Here
are fried scorpions on a stick. And over there are crickets, snakes, duck
tongues, and frogs."

Martin's face grew pale. "Does everyone in China eat those things?" he asked.

"We eat mostly what's produced in our region," Meixiang replied. "In the North,
we grow wheat. So we eat lots of noodles. The great rice fields are in the South."

"But what are you going to eat right now?" Martin asked, sounding worried.

Meixiang thought for a moment. "I'll have a *sienbing,*" she said. "Chinese pizza."

Martin breathed a sigh of relief. "Make that two!"

When they got home, Grandfather Wei showed Martin a photo.

"Is that you and my grandfather when you were young?" Martin asked.

"It certainly is," Grandfather Wei replied. "We explored China together. I'm hoping to take you on the same tour. You'll be able to see what your grandfather saw with your own eyes."

20-21

"An army of eight thousand clay soldiers, larger than life-size and buried in an underground chamber for more than two thousand years!" Martin said. "I wouldn't believe it if I weren't looking at it right now!"

Martin, Meixiang, and Grandfather Wei were visiting the Terracotta Army near the city of Xi'an in central China.

"There are hundreds of clay horses and chariots, too," Grandfather Wei said. "Shi Huangdi, the emperor who united China, had this army built to guard his tomb."

"The Emperor ordered the workers to make every single soldier in the Terracotta Army different," Meixiang added.

"What's that?" Martin asked when he caught sight of something very odd behind one of the soldiers. But it vanished in a split second.

For the rest of the day, Martin couldn't stop thinking about what he'd seen for just an instant—a small green dragon.

22-23

A few days later, Grandfather Wei took Martin and Meixiang to visit the Chengdu Panda Base in south-central China, where scientists were studying and breeding giant pandas and teaching visitors about conservation.

"For giant pandas, nothing is more delicious than bamboo," Meixiang said. "Did you know that they often sleep high up in trees to protect themselves from danger?"

Martin didn't answer because, just then, he saw it again—the green dragon.

Martin couldn't forget the dragon. "Is it real or a dream?" he wondered. "If it's real, is it playing hide and seek with me?" But soon they were off on their next adventure—a trip up the Yangtze River.

24-25

"The Yangtze is the third longest river in the world, and its gorges are truly spectacular," Grandfather Wei said. "We'll go downriver and then we'll travel to the city of Guilin."

"That's where Elephant Trunk Hill is!" shouted Meixiang.

"That's a strange name," Martin said.

"It's a rock on the Li River," Meixiang explained, "shaped like a gigantic elephant drinking. According to legend, some peasants freed the elephant because the emperor was working it to death. The elephant wanted to thank the peasants by staying to help them. But the emperor was furious and turned the elephant into stone while it was drinking from the river."

In the nearby town of Yangshuo, Grandfather Wei rented bamboo rafts for a trip on the Li River to the rice terraces, where at harvest time children help their parents gather the rice.

They were on the river when Martin saw something moving underneath his sweater. He heard a scrambling noise—and out it jumped. The green dragon!

"Yikes!" Martin yelled as he tumbled into the water. "This is not a dream!"

26-27

But perhaps it was a dream.
The dragon didn't reappear in the
ancient city of Suzhou where Martin,
Meixiang, and Grandfather Wei went next.
Their first stop was a large bonsai garden.

"Bonsai is the art of growing tiny trees in
containers or on rocks," Meixiang said.

"This place is super," Martin said. "I feel like a
giant in it!"

At the Suzhou Silk Museum, they saw an exhibit
on how silk worms produce silk. "They feed on mulberry
leaves," Martin was told. "The worms make thin silk threads and
wrap them around their bodies into cocoons. Each thread has to
be unwound to make silk fabric. No wonder silk is so expensive!"

After the museum, Martin, Meixiang, and Grandfather Wei climbed Tiger Hill, famous for its beautiful scenery.

"King Helu is buried on this hill," Grandfather Wei said. "One legend tells of a white tiger that appeared three days after the King's burial and guarded his tomb."

28-29

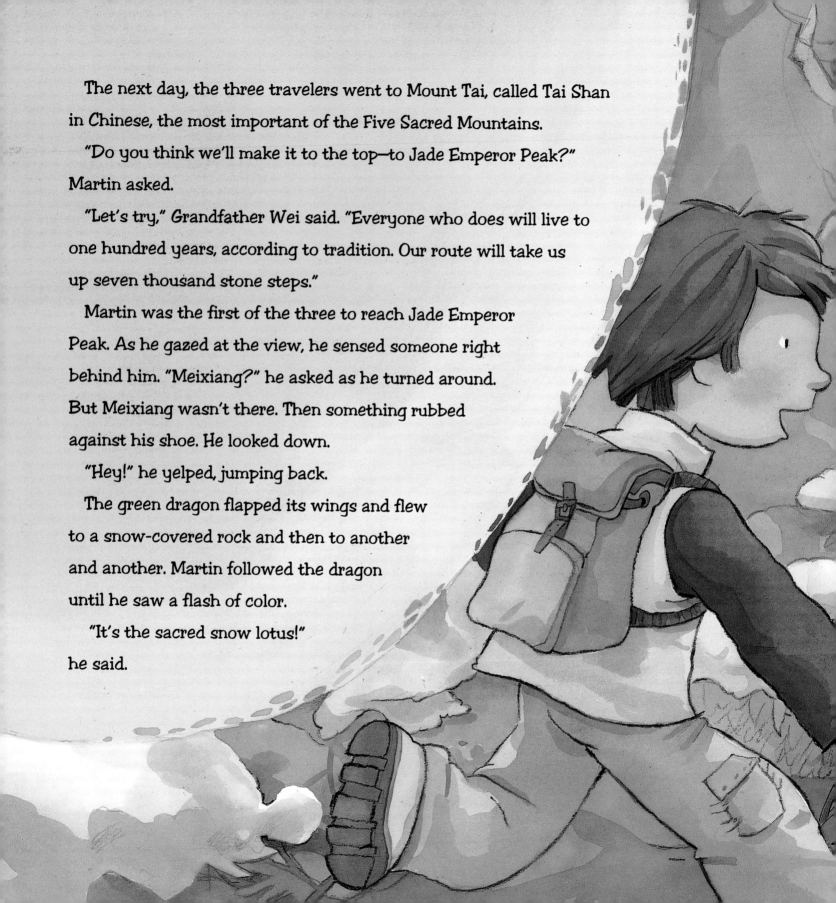

The next day, the three travelers went to Mount Tai, called Tai Shan in Chinese, the most important of the Five Sacred Mountains.

"Do you think we'll make it to the top—to Jade Emperor Peak?" Martin asked.

"Let's try," Grandfather Wei said. "Everyone who does will live to one hundred years, according to tradition. Our route will take us up seven thousand stone steps."

Martin was the first of the three to reach Jade Emperor Peak. As he gazed at the view, he sensed someone right behind him. "Meixiang?" he asked as he turned around. But Meixiang wasn't there. Then something rubbed against his shoe. He looked down.

"Hey!" he yelped, jumping back.

The green dragon flapped its wings and flew to a snow-covered rock and then to another and another. Martin followed the dragon until he saw a flash of color.

"It's the sacred snow lotus!" he said.

Grandfather Wei had told Martin that this lotus
is supposed to have healing powers. He knew that
some people also believed that if you drank the
dew inside the flower, you would have a long life
of wisdom. He got his travel flask out of his
backpack and collected the drops of dew. He
looked around for the dragon, but it was gone.

Martin heard Meixiang and Grandfather Wei
coming up the path. He quickly walked away from
the flower so they wouldn't see it. Meixiang had
once said, "If you reveal where you've found a
snow lotus, it will vanish beneath the snow."

"Do you want a sip of water?" Martin asked Meixiang, holding out his flask.

After Meixiang drank a little of the dew, Martin finished the last few drops. As he put away his flask, he noticed that Grandfather Wei was smiling.

"Has he guessed that I found the snow lotus?" Martin asked himself.

32-33

The next morning Martin said good-bye to Meixiang and Grandfather Wei.

"Remember," they said, "good friends are close even when they are far apart."

Martin was sad to leave them, but he knew that finding the sacred snow lotus marked the end of his journey in China. He hiked up to a lookout point on the mountain and put his magic necklace around his neck. He took a deep breath—and something tapped him on the shoulder.

It was the small green dragon! It had been hiding in his backpack.

Martin couldn't help laughing. "What game are you playing—now you see me, now you don't?" The dragon seemed to nod. "And what am I supposed to do now?" Martin asked. "Take you with me?" The dragon seemed to nod again.

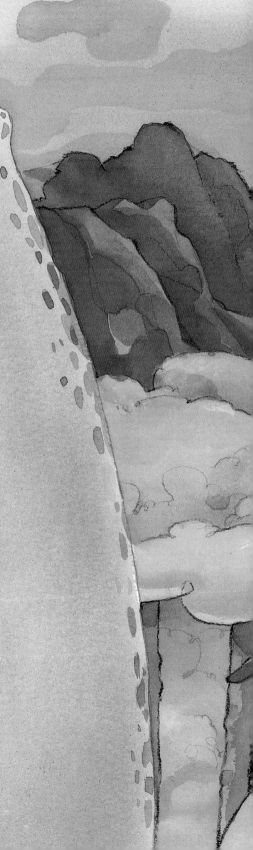

"Okay," Martin said, "but you need a name. How about . . . *See-me?*"

The dragon looked satisfied. So Martin closed his eyes and said, *"HOME!"*

1,2,3 suddenly in
# CHINA
The Sacred Flower

First edition for the United States and Canada published
in 2011 by Barron's Educational Series, Inc.
© Copyright 2010 by Gemser Publications, S.L.
C/Castell, 38; Teià (08329) Barcelona, Spain (World Rights)
Author: Cristina Falcón Maldonado
Adaptation of English Text: Joanne Barkan
Illustrator: Marta Fàbrega

All rights reserved. No part of this publication may be
reproduced or distributed in any form or by any means
without the written permission of the copyright owner.

*All inquiries should be addressed to:*
Barron's Educational Series, Inc.
250 Wireless Boulevard
Hauppauge, NY 11788
**www.barronseduc.com**

ISBN-13: 978-0-7641-4583-4
ISBN-10: 0-7641-4583-5

Library of Congress Control No.: 2010931206

Date of Manufacture: December 2010
Manufactured by: L. Rex Printing, Tin Wan, Aberdeen, Hong Kong

Printed in China
9 8 7 6 5 4 3 2 1

# GLOSSARY

**YEAR OF THE DRAGON:** The Year of the Dragon is a year of good
luck. People born under the sign of the dragon are considered to be
noble, wise, creative, and supportive.
The Chinese calendar consists of twelve annual cycles, each one
corresponding to an animal: Rat, ox, tiger, rabbit, monkey, dragon,
snake, ram, horse, rooster, dog, and pig. Each person is assigned
with a sign depending on the year in which they were born. (Page 5)

**NI HAO:** Hello in Mandarin Chinese, the official language
of China. (Page 7)

**PEKING DUCK:** One of China's national dishes. Its name refers to the
old name given to the country's capital city, Peking (today's Beijing).
The dish is roast duck, traditionally eaten with pancakes, spring onions,
and *haisin* sauce. (Page 17)

**XIN NIAN KUAI LE:** Congratulations and prosperity. (Page 12)

**RICKSHAW:** A bicycle taxi or cart driven by the rider. It's a very
common means of transport in Beijing. (Page 14)

**TAI-CHI:** A very ancient martial art, consisting in gentle harmonious
movements, highly beneficial for physical and mental health. (Page 14)